Emily and Her Monkey Plant a Garden

by Patricia Ryan and Emily Grossman
Illustrated by Emily Grossman

WARNER
JUVENILE
BOOKS

A Warner Communications Company
New York

Suggested for readers ages 5 and up.

Warner Juvenile Books Edition
Copyright © 1989 by Patricia Ryan and Emily Grossman
All rights reserved.
Warner Early Reader™ is a trademark of Warner Books, Inc.
Warner Books, Inc., 666 Fifth Avenue, New York, NY 10103

A Warner Communications Company

Printed in Italy

First Warner Juvenile Books Printing: May 1989
10 9 8 7 6 5 4 3 2 1

Library of Congress Cataloging-in-Publication Data

Ryan, Patricia
    Emily and her monkey plant a garden.

    Summary: In Emily's dream, she and her toy monkey
surprise Grandpa with vegetables that she planted,
watered, and picked.
    [1. Vegetable gardening—Fiction.   2. Gardening—
Fiction]   I. Grossman, Emily, ill.   II. Title.
PZ7.R9554En   1989   [E]   88-21605
ISBN 1-55782-054-6

This is Emily.

This is her toy monkey.

Emily likes to eat vegetables.

Emily likes the vegetables that her grandpa grows in his garden best of all!

That night, Emily dreams that she and her toy monkey plant their very own garden, where they grow only their favorite things.

"First," Emily explains to her monkey, "we have to pick a place where the vegetables will grow well . . .

and that means lots of sunshine."

Emily and her monkey go to the gardening store to buy their supplies.

They buy one shovel, one rake and two spades.

The most fun of all is picking out the seeds!

They pick carrots, peppers, lettuce, corn and tomatoes.

"And for Halloween," says Emily, "pumpkins!"

"Before we plant our seeds," Emily tells her monkey, "we have to use our tools to clear the ground. First, we'll use the shovel to turn over the soil and make it soft. Then we'll use the rake to smooth the ground for even rows. And with the spade we'll dig tiny holes for the seeds."

Then Emily and her monkey plant the seeds,
evenly, row by row.

Then they water the seeds.

And then they wait.

And wait.

And wait.

Finally, the vegetables are ready to be picked!

Emily and her monkey pick the vegetables.

Emily and her monkey can't wait to give Grandpa some vegetables from *their* very own garden!

"Today would be a good day to plant a garden—
just like the one in my dream!"